The Same Deep Water as You

by

Chad Lutzke

Introduction

Welcome to the world of author Chad Lutzke. I say world because Chad isn't just writing stories, he's creating a universe. Each book seems interconnected in one big Lutzkian web.

I don't mean cute little Easter eggs where references, characters, or plot-lines reference one another. I mean there is a deeper unifying element in the emotions of each story, the journey of each character. His collection is one big song—a rhapsody, in which the human spirit comes face to face with the horrors of the world, and the readers cheer them on through the rite of passage. No character ends the way they start in a Lutzke story. Nor does a reader. Every book leaves its mark. Sacred truths like love and redemption are not clichés but attainable, and there is faith that we can survive the darkness the world has to offer, certainly with our battle wounds, but better off for facing the challenge.

Chad—and I say 'Chad' because he's the kind of writer you call by his first name, for his books strip down all pretense and convention and are so personal—writes within the horror realm, but he offers kindness rather than slaughter, and this is something to be celebrated, heralded. He doesn't just stick an axe in his character's chest, but reaches into the chest of the readers', caresses their heart, massages each valve, and shows them what's inside. There is an ever-present empathy for the human predicament, and a sense of sweetness. Sweetness might seem an odd word since his books include such creative darkness: a neglected 12-year-old lives with his mother's decaying body, an older teen with a skull for a face travels across the country, an aging man loses the love of his life but falls in love with an identical cadaver, but it is sweetness you will find. This is all the more admirable, for even within the dark mind of the author, he still celebrates the glow of the human spirit.

Perhaps it's no coincidence that things seem to often be 'decaying' in Chad's works—a negligent parent, one's own face, or the body of a loved one. We journey on toward something greater even among the decay, searching for meaning while we are busy dying. No matter who you are, decay is coming, and Chad never lets us forget.

The title itself—In the Same Deep Water as You—showcases Chad's empathy for the human predicament, one in which we all travel through our own personal journey but on shared paths, and this book drips with precision in all the right places. While not a piece of horror, if you know Chad from the horror genre, where his name seems to appear everywhere, you'll love this one. Don't flinch when the shiny glint of a sharp blade appears, sparkling above the water, or when the human skull falls upon unforgiving pavement. But what matters most is the emotion of the hero's journey, which at its core is just to be accepted, loved and to feel worthy. Pathetic clichés in some writer's hands, but something to root for in Chad's.

In Water, Chad both writes from the wound and from that place of hope, and like many of his books, the yearnings of youth are showcased. In Water, it is a quest for love amongst the potential evils of lust, to find a partner that affirms one's existence and doesn't stifle it with jealousy and self-destruction. Nothing gold can stay, but it still can shine at the end. Moments of this book will sneak up on you—my jaw dropped more than once as I read—because he's tapped into a world we all know so well. You'll no doubt recognize your own group of friends, a mix of lost slackers with varying degrees of idealism and shifting morality, wandering through each day looking for adventure, pulling youthful pranks at times, and jumping to deadly whims at others.

The youthful sentimentality of the story was inspired and guided by the music of The Cure. Fans will notice this in the chapter titles, as well as sprinkles of dialogue inspired by their lyrics. The power of a song to spark a memory, to evoke emotion that is only recognized in certain octaves, is something Chad nails in this work. There is a melancholy reminiscing in Water that captures The Cure, and there's a narrative here you can feel is close to Chad's heart.

Music is such a universal experience, life given a voice. The shared experience of a song is nothing less than spiritual. We all know what it is like to re-experience an emotion soon as we hear that first note. Despite this transcendence, it is experienced in solitude. No person experiences a song exactly the same way. And some of us hear notes that the others do not, like the hero's journey in Chad's books, they travel a road just like ours, but each of them on their own, and with each their own soundtrack.

Welcome to the world of Chad Lutzke, a place where you will want to live. And after reading his works, you will realize you already do.

-Mark Matthews, author of Milk-Blood and Body of Christ, December 2018

"Love is patient, love is kind. It does not envy, it does not boast, it is not proud. It does not dishonor others, it is not self-seeking, it is not easily angered, it keeps no record of wrongs. Love does not delight in evil but rejoices with the truth. It always protects, always trusts, always hopes, always perseveres."

~ 1 Corinthians 13:4-7

Lust: 1. Intense sexual desire.

a. An overwhelming desire or craving

b. Intense eagerness or enthusiasm

Plainsong

It was early spring, and we were kept warm by the humming heater as snow fell outside the car. The snow. There's warmth in it somehow, isn't there? Have you ever lain in the deep snow and felt the contentment it brings? Like a mother's embrace willing you to sleep. It's entrancing. And at night it's like the stars are falling. Coming in for a wet kiss.

That's how it was that night in Jessica's car.

A picture of Jesus hung from her keys, jutting out from the ignition while we parked in front of my apartment. The picture was a famous painting. One that I was probably more familiar with than her. For her it was the default keychain she never replaced.

The radio was there instead of conversation. It was saying more than we ever could. Offering melodies and lyrics that spoke for us. And in this way we were connected. Though in her mind, she may have been holding my hand, her tongue in my mouth. And that's where our connection stops.

I imagine the ache in her stomach she must have felt. A longing that screamed inside her while the tranquilizing snow fell from an ink-black sky, the lyrics preaching love to her and peace to me. Like a church service, the pews filled with different perspectives. One attendee walks out with a newfound strength to leave an unhealthy relationship, another finds forgiveness for a sin that's haunted them for years, and yet another deems it a good day to start over, begin anew.

For me the moment was euphoric. But not because of her. A spiritual connection was being made. But not with her. With the soundtrack, and with the moment. And with the memory of that cold spring night that would bleed into summer. A summer that would end in lament.

Untitled

1.

Jessica didn't always get along with others, particularly girls. She was abrasive, intimidating and assertive. Her honesty was brutal. She'd be the first to tell a complete stranger their fly was down, that there was food between their teeth. But I could handle her. For me it was part of her charm. That and the Robert Smith goth mop she wore so well, bright red lips and raccoon eyes. Even if I didn't really get it, it was different. And I respect anyone with individuality, with self expression that doesn't follow a trend.

I met her through Allen. She'd come to watch him skate, something we did with every waking hour that year. And the year before. She made fun of my long hair, called me a hessian. Something I'd learn later was vulgar slang for metalhead, which didn't make sense since metal wasn't really my thing. Punk rock was. Hardcore. The long hair was for the chicks. It got me a lot of them, and I was too vain to shave my head. Allen had a devilock—shaved head, all but the lengthy bangs that hung over his face. She didn't make fun of that.

Jessica had a friend with her that day. Someone who wasn't goth but just as abrasive, just as intimidating, but much more assertive and with a nose so ugly it was attractive. Makes no sense, I know. Like chicks with a snaggletooth or a gap in their teeth. Cute, aren't they? Her name was Vera.

I remember I skated well that day, landed nearly everything. There's something about a chick watching you that makes it easy, keeps the board under you. But I was feeling good in general anyway, a foreign thing around that time. I'd just ended a lengthy relationship and was still getting over it. You know how it is. Never in your life have you seen so many gray Monte Carlos until the two of you are through. Then they're everywhere and you've got one eye on the street and the other on life ahead, trying to keep your shit together. Especially around friends. Nobody likes the guy who can't shut up about his ex.

So, we were skating in the parking lot of a plaza when the jocks showed up, crowbars in hand

14

and chasing after us. It happened often. Jealousy is my guess. Here we are, these counter culture folks wearing what we please, unconcerned with the latest trends. Unconcerned about the pressure of fitting in, the size of our dicks in the shower after the game. It spells freedom and identity. Jocks and preps, they hate that shit. It scares the hell out of them. Because it's everything they wish they could be. Add in a couple cuties on the sidelines watching the freaks do their thing, popping tricks they'll never be able to do, and the testosterone fuels rage.

We sprinted for Jessica's car, jocks screaming from behind. I had no idea which car was hers until I saw her jump into this little red Fiero, and I'm thinking we're screwed. How the hell are we going to pile into this thing? A two-seater. At least one of us is going down. But we did it, boards in hand. Allen grabbed the passenger seat and I climbed in, sat right in his lap, and a crowbar went flying. I slammed the door shut and steel hit the door, leaving a giant dent that could have been any one of our heads. I looked back for Vera and she's just standing there against her own car. Her clothes are prep camouflage. They want nothing to do with her beautiful, ugly nose. They just want the hessian and the devilock. To bring our heads back to their Izod tribe of narrow-minded goons who drink heavy on the weekends in between games, where they grab ass and share kiss-and-tell stories.

Anyway, that's how I met Jessica. And that's the first time she saved me.

2.

We hit it off, Jessica and I. She'd show up at skating sessions, her and Vera. Looking back, she was a bad omen when it came to getting jumped, because she was there the next time too. Completely different place, completely different jocks. No crowbar this time, just muscle busting through tank tops like string-wrapped hams. They took out my buddy, Begman. Knocked him out cold while we scattered every which way like roaches when the kitchen light comes on. Poor bastard.

By just being a friend, Jessica kind of saved me a second time. Someone to take my mind off the ex—a girl I thought I'd marry. That was the plan, anyway. But you don't really know how to treat a girl when you're 19. It's like trial and error and nothing gets figured out until it's too late. When you're 19 you're selfish and for the life of you can't figure out the difference between love and lust.

Having Jessica as a friend took that warm heart a girl can offer and left out the sex, the romance, and the jealousy. No love. No lust. I valued that.

It turns out that little red Fiero—that escape pod—wasn't really her car. Her dad owned a dealership, and for a while she'd drive a different car every day, until she finally settled on a four-door. Much better for getting away, keeping our skulls intact when the crowbars come out.

We put a lot of miles into that car, driving around town mostly. Or parked and talking. Those were miles, too. Hours of both philosophical and brainless chatter in clouds of cigarette smoke. That's when we'd listen to The Cure. It was the perfect soundtrack for a budding relationship between two friends—a goth and a hessian. A soundtrack that took

17

snapshots, kept them safe, then showed them off when played again years later. Spring snow, midsummer moonlight, the serene ripple of water, the beach under an ebony sky, and a plethora of streetlights. They're locked into those songs. They are one now, and always will be. The melodies conjure the surroundings, and the memories they bring are both joyful and somber. I just put the record on and I'm there. You get it. You've got your own soundtrack. One for each year.

3.

We were at Allen's Uncle's house a lot. It was a place to drink beer and laugh. Don was a Vietnam veteran who's seen a shit-ton and has episodes where he's not himself. He's off in the jungle with his back to the wall, and if you ever catch him sleeping you don't ever wake him up. His girlfriend did once and he broke her face with a socket wrench, put her in the hospital. But for the most part, Don is on the level. He's good people. He's the kind of guy who's reckless with everything he does. Loaded with scars.

18

Beat-up hands with blackened nails from too many misses with a hammer or getting smashed by car parts. A real hard-working man. One that works hard at never having to work for the man. Odd jobs like hauling trash, stripping things for copper, flipping cars. A lot of hard work just to avoid hard work.

Don also grew marijuana in his bathroom, surrounded by lights and tin foil. I'd quit smoking weed the year before or I may have found it cool. His bathroom was like pissing in the woods under an electric sun.

One night Allen, Jessica, Vera, Begman and I were hanging out at Uncle Don's, drinking beer and watching this shitty TV of his—complete with rabbit ears and foil—when Vera started in.

"You guys hear about Tara Miller?" She puffed on her cigarette. We puffed on ours.

"I know she's a crackhead now," Allen said through a breath of smoke.

"She was raped."

"Isn't she a prostitute?" Begman asked.

"It doesn't mean she deserves to get raped."

19

"I know. I was just sayin'..." Begman kinda turtled out of the conversation after that. He was an awkward guy but a loyal friend. Unless given the chance to talk shit behind your back, then he'd make a day of it. He was married to his board, and we couldn't figure out if he was gay or just asexual. Either way we didn't give a shit. He was an asset to the group. Good sense of humor, nonconformist, and had a real passion for skating. That guy loved his board more than any of us and vowed to never give it up no matter how old he was. It was easy to believe.

"Who told you that?" I asked.

"Her mom. I saw her at the store, loading up on booze."

"The hell she tell you that for? Why would she tell anyone? It's none of our business."

"Geez, don't shoot the messenger."

"I just don't think it's the kind of thing that should be thrown out there, especially by her own mother. Damn."

"He was wearing a ski mask."

Jessica sat close and held my hand, like I was protecting her somehow.

"I'm hungry," Allen said. "Can we hit this cereal, Uncle Don?" He pointed toward the kitchen counter that held four boxes of the same cereal. Batman.

"Hell no you can't. I'm selling those one day. They'll be some comic-book kid's wet dream."

Allen had already known the answer. He just liked to get a rise out of people, get a laugh at their expense. Sometimes it was funny. This was one of those times. And we all laughed at the thought of holding onto so much cereal with the hopes of making a buck off it someday.

* * *

Later that night an old friend stopped by Uncle Don's. I hadn't seen John in a few years. He looked good, healthy, and had chopped off his mohawk. John asked if I wanted to step outside and have a chat. I grabbed my beer and cigarettes and we headed out. It was dark and the woods surrounding the house made it darker.

John asked how I was doing and I told him I was on the mend from a broken heart but not bad otherwise. He pointed to the beer in my hand and said "You don't have to do that, you know...live like this." Then he gave me a hug and told me he loved me and told me God loved me. I said thanks and we went back inside.

It was weird, considering the year before our bands played a show together and he'd gotten into a fight, put some guy's head through a window. John had really changed, and I couldn't stop thinking about what he said. I thought about it all night, especially while standing alone, pissing in the marijuana jungle.

Fascination Street

1.

We skated a lot. We'd grab our boards and go all over town, hitting our favorite spots. One day it was me, Allen, Begman, Maurice and Rocco. This was how it usually was. Maurice couldn't skate for shit but he had a car and was fun to be around. Plus he always had cigarettes. Maurice lost his dad not even a year before and now he and his mom were real close. He'd call her every few hours and check in. Nineteen years old. We'd tease him about it, but none of us really got it. We loved the freedom from our parents, but we all had fathers, mothers. None of us took the time to grasp his situation. Instead, we teased him for being a momma's boy.

We ended up at the mall where Rocco and Allen got into it in the parking lot. I'm not even sure what they were going on about, but I thought it would come to blows at one point, right there in the back seat. Rocco got out of the car to blow off steam, pop some ollies. The rest of us stayed in, finished our cigarettes. Then Allen whipped his junk out and pissed in Rocco's Pepsi. Rocco got back in the car and nobody said a word. We just watched with bit tongues as he took a swig. Drank that piss-pop right down and thought nothing of it.

We went in the mall and walked around. Not to shop, but to people watch. I was there to scope out chicks, praying I didn't run into my ex.

Every once in a while we'd lay down our boards and hit the steps, then pick up like nothing ever happened. We were used to getting kicked out of just about everywhere, but never the mall. Either we were too sneaky or they just didn't care.

I flirted with a girl and got her number but forgot her name so I wrote down "Jeff" next to it. She had these eyebrows that made her eyes look cat-like. Our friend Jeff had those same eyebrows.

Rocco had money and bought us all pretzels. It made me feel bad that I'd sat and watched him drink that piss-Pepsi.

We went to the record store and checked out the hardcore section. They had Agnostic Front, GBH, English Dogs, C.O.C, and Crumbsuckers on vinyl for

$2 each. Maurice let me run out to the car and scrounge it for money. That car was always full of change, most of the time enough for a pack of smokes or a bagful of burgers. I found $12 and bought the records.

We caught wind of a show over in Cascade Hills—a rich part of town, where all the girls were nice and pretty and the preps holed away in their trophy-filled rooms. Driveways filled with cars Mom and Dad bought. A few of my favorite locals were playing: Broken Trust and The Sinatras. We showed up and skated in the street before the show. Begman broke his board trying to land something and threw a fit. He's a peaceful guy, a pacifist, but he got scary for a minute there throwing the broken 7-ply around and screaming about it. His board was his life. Maurice felt self conscious in his square clothes, so he went home to change. I told him it didn't matter, but he got it in his head that if he's going to a punk show then he needs to look the part. He showed back up with ripped jeans that had "U2" written in marker on his leg. He would have been better off in khakis and a button-up.

2.

Allen was over at my place. He brought 40s with him. We downed them and wrote some songs. I was in this situation where you've got a good friend and you want him in your band but he can't play an instrument for shit, so you stick a mic in his hand and hope it works. It did. He was good with it, got the pit going, but wrote stupid lyrics. Songs like "Nicotine Penis." Nothing but a joke.

My landlady showed up, said she could smell weed coming from my place. I hadn't smoked that shit in a year, but there was no convincing her. Then she asked if I would come next door and take a look at her water heater. I said sure, and Allen and I put our best sober suits on and followed her. Taking those careful steps you take when you're trying hard to pull off that you're not two 40s deep.

I poked at the water heater, like you do when you're under the hood of a car and don't have a clue

27

what you're doing. You're just tugging at wires, twisting caps, wiggling shit around. Allen and I both held back laughing. I told her I didn't know what was wrong with it and said she should call a repairman, that it was out of my league. We laughed all the way back to my place.

3.

We made stickers for the band at the print shop and plastered them all over town. On store windows, deposit boxes at the bank drive-thru, on the trashcans in the mall. Then Maurice got some spray paint from his house and we hit every skate spot with the band name in bright pink letters. Marking our territory.

Later that night we played a basement show. The band that played before us had a drummer with a cage to hold his kit. It was ridiculous and took an hour to set up and tear down. He thought he was Neil Peart or something.

There were too many people there, and Allen sung half the show being held up by the crowd, like a

28

king on a flesh throne. The guy who owned the PA stood next to his gear all night, protecting it. The whole time with this worried look on his face. He was in a heavy metal band and had never been to a punk show before. When we were done playing, I heard him mumble something about never letting us use his stuff again. He made me want to shave my head.

A lot of curious folks showed up, looking for beer, raising an eyebrow at the music. The house was full of cheerleader types I'd gone to school with. Chicks that never gave me the time of day. I spent the rest of the night making out with one of them in a big, cushioned chair while people sat around us and drank. I thought a crowbar might come down on me at any moment. It would have been worth it.

4.

When we weren't driving around listening to The Cure, Jessica and I would be at my apartment, playing bad video games on a tiny black and white TV. But it made for good times. She'd become my best friend. One time I came out of the store with her favorite candy bar and this cheap-ass plastic flower, gave it to her. She hugged me and said, "I love you, Jex...you're my best friend," then gave me a quick kiss on the lips. And from then on that was our thing, expressing that kind of love. A simple kiss and a simple *I love you* between two best friends.

Sometimes Jessica would stay the night and we'd share my bed while the city lulled us to sleep through an open window. If our relationship weren't platonic, I suppose it would have been romantic. But it wasn't. Not for me.

5.

Two weeks into April and it was snowing. We spent the day hitting the secondary spots, less-than-stellar areas that held no decent benches, no rails, no banks or curbs. We got bored and Maurice went home to be with his mom while Jessica drove me, Allen, and Begman around. We met up with Vera and her new boyfriend Nathan. He was a lifeguard at the local beach. A guy that tried really hard to be a hippie. The beads, the sandals, the dead stickers on his Volkswagen bus. He was real laid back and seemed cool, but that hippie shit I just couldn't take seriously.

We followed them to the west side of town for a party. I get quiet at these things. I'm not myself. I've never considered myself an introvert, but parties bring that out in me. Faking smiles, mingling with people I don't know. And if I'm sober, forget it. I'm no fun. I'm like Maurice, awkward and shit.

It was freezing out, and I was hugging myself to keep warm because I was too cool to wear a coat. The fact I was wearing shorts didn't help either. My way of denying the weather. We got to the party and it was in a garage. No windows, just a side door. The door opened and light spilled out onto the moonlit snow, turning it from blue to yellow-orange. It's like the sun was being kept in that garage. Then I felt the warmth. There were heat lamps and space heaters in every corner, and the whole garage was filled with sand. I mean every inch of it. The walls were lined with lawn chairs filled with penny-loafing jocks and tan-legged cheerleader types, cups of beer in hand. I didn't want to be there, but the heat drew me in and I followed Allen, Begman and Jessica. Vera and Nathan already mingling. This was their scene.

I sat in a chair next to Jessica, and she smiled at people she knew, waving. I didn't know anybody. Except for one person. Morgan, my ex. She saw me at the same time and we both had this frozen look on our faces like what the hell do we do now. Do we smile? Do we pretend we don't know each other? Do we scowl and look away? I was sure she could see my heart pumping through my chest, see my face go pale and hear my stomach eat itself.

Jessica saw it all and said, "Is that her?"

"Yeah."

"Bitch."

I spotted the keg in the corner but couldn't move.

Begman leaned into me and said "Dude…"

"I know, man. I know."

The sand on the floor was deep, and everyone had their shoes off, barefoot, toes digging in the sand. But I was too cool to do that, not with people I didn't know. Not with Morgan sitting across from me. Her shoes were off too, and her nails were painted pink. Other toes were touching hers—the guy next to her. Long blonde hair, skinny. The asshole looked just like me. *Hessian*, I thought.

Jessica got up and grabbed us each a beer. It felt like high school. There was division. The jocks and the preps. Then the skater punks. I drank my beer and wondered if any of the jocks in the room had jumped us before. Or maybe just not yet.

I had a couple more beers before we left, and it took everything I had not to walk across the pseudo beach and ask Morgan to go outside, where I'd make an ass of myself, asking what went wrong between us and could it ever work again. But I knew it was over. And not because her hand made its way into another that night. But because deep down I didn't want it to work. I drew a line in the sand between love and lust, and I was one step further to figuring shit out.

* * *

We ended up at Uncle Don's where we sat in the dark and talked about how another girl had been raped and they think it was the same guy. When the term serial rapist came up, I shut the rest of the conversation out and thought about the cereal on the counter and how hungry I was. Four unopened boxes of shitty cereal. A comic-book kid's wet dream.

6.

Jessica picked me up and took me to where her mother worked, wanted me to meet her. She was a sweetheart of a woman with a frisky side and took to me right away. She worked at the hospital so we wandered the halls for a while, saw a guy laid out on a stretcher who'd gotten hit in the face real good. His lips were swollen and splotchy with red dots. They reminded me of Apple Jacks cereal. He was in a lot of pain, totally out of it. And I wondered if a crowbar ever catches up with me is that what I'll look like. Apple Jacks cereal.

Jessica dropped me off at Allen's where Maurice picked us up. He had to run an errand for his mom, get something from the mall. While there, we passed the candle store and I locked eyes with a cute brunette working the counter. She wouldn't look away and neither would I. But that's all it was, looking. Being shy wasn't some kind of game I played. I just couldn't talk to girls for shit—not sober anyway—unless they approached me first. So we just traded ridiculous, long, exaggerated smiles and I kept on walking.

We stopped at Maurice's house. He ran in, checked in with his mom, then brought me and Allen bottles of Pepsi and said he called Begman and Rocco and they wanted to skate.

When we got to Rocco's he was stoned. He was like that a lot, either weed or acid. And over the course of just a few years I watched him get slower. He talked slower, skated slower, and couldn't remember shit. It was sad and one of the reasons I quit smoking pot altogether. His older brother dealt weed and acid so it was always around. I hated his brother for that, for the slowing down of Rocco.

We got to Begman's and sat in his driveway, honking the horn while NWA played on the stereo. I hated that shit, and every chance I got I'd slip in some Minor Threat or The Accused while we were out. I figured we may as well listen to something we all liked. I'd heard enough about South Central, Compton, and every other ghetto. It was the only music I'd ever heard that made people change the way they walk and talk. You get a kid listening to rap who's got no self identity and before long he's all slurs with a hard front and a Triple F.A.T. Goose, completely forgetting his roots. One year they're driving around the car Mom and Dad bought them, the next they think they're from South Central. Dick in one hand, a 40 of malt in the other. Posers.

"I'll get him," Maurice said.

"No, stay here," Allen said. "Beg can't have people in the house."

"Why's that?"

"Cuz his dad likes to dress in women's clothes. But don't tell him I told you."

"No shit?"

"Yeah, but don't say anything."

Begman came out right then, cap on his head and a new board in hand. The second he got in the car, Maurice spilled it.

"Your dad dresses like a chick?"

"What the hell, man?" Allen yelled.

Begman looked right at Allen. "Dick...Hey, Rocco. Allen pissed in your Pepsi when we were at the mall."

"Bullshit," Rocco said, then saw Allen fighting a smile. "Did I drink it?"

"Bigtime," Begman said.

"Payback's a bitch, asshole."

* * *

We hit McKinley School—our favorite spot. Giant asphalt humps and cement benches in the middle of a playground. Begman broke in his new board. By the time we were done the graphics were gone. It was good to see him so happy. We stacked three and four boards at the top of the humps, taking turns clearing them. Maurice bought us all burgers and Faygo and we ate under the sun, ass on boards. He had to bail home to his mom so the rest of us stayed, then headed downtown.

Once we got downtown, some dude walked by with a brick in his hand. He didn't like it too much that we were skating and told us so. We stood with our boards in hand while the dude talked shit, and I could tell at any minute he'd swing that brick. I imagined hitting him across the face with my board, taking him right out. But sometimes I think too much about consequences. What ifs. What if I hit him too hard, he smacks on the pavement and never walks again? We just rode away from the prick, his voice getting louder. Eventually he threw the brick but missed.

It started raining so we broke into an abandoned factory, moved some stuff around inside, made some makeshift boxes to grind on. It was dark in there and the ground was covered in old machine oil, but it beat skating in the rain. Rain was the devil. It meant you had to make do with what you had.

Parking garages, abandoned buildings. Snow and the cold were even worse. It was like trying to quit smoking for a season. You're always thinking about it, needing it, but you're broke so you're out there looking for butts on the ground, puffing away on them even though they taste like shit.

But summer had just begun.

7.

We were skating at the bank, hitting the two-step handrail, when up rides Aaron. He was an awkward guy we barely knew, with a nest of hair that could pass for a wig. We'd see him out skating some of the Lakeview spots, but rarely downtown.

"I got an idea," he said. "You guys wanna skate down there?" He pointed to an electronics store down the road. "There's a gap behind it."

We got down there and the place was loaded with pebbles and dirt. We spent twenty minutes just clearing it away. It was a tough gap, with not much room to build enough speed to clear it. We'd have to skate alongside the building on the walk, make a little turn, then launch. The gap itself was a large patch of grass between the walk and the parking lot. None of us made it, but we got close enough to keep trying. An hour later we gave up. That turn just before the launch was killing the land.

We sat in the grass we'd been trying to clear and split a Mountain Dew, lit some smokes. Then out of nowhere Aaron asked what we'd do if our kid was being molested by someone. The easy answer was we'd beat the shit out of them. But the bigger question was why he'd ask something like that. He never told us, just grabbed his board and said, "I got an idea," then left.

We never skated with Aaron again after that. Weeks later he was in prison for beating a guy to death. And you know how rumors go. There's always more than one. The first being he killed a guy for molesting his girlfriend's kid. The other that his girl was an older woman into occult shit and put it in Aaron's head that her ex needed to die. Love makes you do some crazy shit. Then again, so does lust.

8.

It was my birthday, so I threw a party at my friend Michelle's house. Technically she was another ex. We went out for a few months when I was 17, she was 23. That's exciting stuff for a teenager, being with an older woman. But she turned into a drunken mess and things went from a fun, cradle-robbing affair to me playing big brother, as she spent her days in a bottle. Baggage I wasn't interested in. But we remained friends, and it became a strange thing to even consider we'd ever been intimate. It's a shame all romantic relationships can't end up like that, instead of the animosity and bitterness that takes over, then remains.

I invited the usual group, plus a few others, and got a pony keg that was empty before the night was through. Michelle spent most of the evening with eyes on my friend Eddie, who wasn't so much scared of her as he was turned off by her drunkenly aggressive seduction. Maurice on the other hand, he was all about trying to impress her. She'd become his mission.

After there were only a handful of us left, we played strip poker. I lost pretty bad. So when I got up to piss, stripped naked, I came out of the bathroom with my watch wrapped around my junk and asked if anyone had the time. Really this was for the guys. Sometimes it's hard to pass on a good joke. Begman and Eddie couldn't breathe for a while after that.

Maurice was relentless in his pursuit of Michelle, so when he finally passed out we carried him to her bedroom and stuck a condom filled with raw egg into his pants. The next day he woke up convinced he'd blacked out and gotten lucky. Lost his virginity and couldn't even remember.

9.

Allen, Begman and I stayed at Maurice's house, stayed up all night playing video games. Never even slept. I hadn't done that since I was a kid. That shit's hard to do when you're older, and the next day is one big hangover.

Maurice and his mom had stuff to do so we had him drop us off at the mall. Bad idea. Walking through the mall on no sleep isn't fun. It's disorienting, and every person in the place annoys the hell out of you. The benches there were long and padded, more like couches, so we spent a lot of time on them, people watching and wishing we were home in bed.

I saw the chick at the candle store again. It was clear she was into me, sent all the signals that were easy to read. But I did nothing, just walked on by and thought about her all day.

Maurice picked us up six hours later. We were miserable, and I never wanted to see the mall again. I had him drop me off at my place and slept the rest of the day. Until Jessica woke me up, climbing into bed. She smelled like makeup and hairspray.

"Another girl was raped downtown," she whispered.

I put my arm around her like I thought she might need it, then we fell asleep.

10.

Allen's grandparents went out of town for the weekend. They wanted him to house sit, so he threw a party. A bunch of us were there. I invited my ex. Not Morgan, but Nicole—the one before her. She broke my heart, too. Well, we broke each other.

We had turned into one of those couples who fight a lot. All the trust was gone, and I became the jealous type. You can't go on like that. We were fine when we were together. But on the phone we were different people. She was cold and distant, pushing me away. I knew what that meant. She'd already started with a wandering eye, ready to bail out should something better come along. It got me feeling insecure, so I shut down. And while Maurice's mom was away on a two-week trip with friends, I stayed at his place and didn't tell Nicole. It's a game guys play sometimes. When things look bad, we make the first move and bail. But it's not the end. Not yet. Because it's a bluff. It's a desperate attempt at gaining control again, getting back that security. When your girlfriend starts worrying, starts crying over you, then you've got them. They begin re-thinking things and you're no longer the weak one. It's a dick move, and it doesn't always work. You get yourself a strong, independent type and she won't go for that shit. So when you bail, you're only doing her a favor, and she's onto better things and never looks back.

For the two weeks I stayed at Maurice's place, I didn't call Nicole once, and she stalked me. Kept calling my apartment, stopping by. Even called Maurice looking for me. The game was working. I had the control. But in those two weeks, I met Morgan and jumped from one to the other. That ain't love. You don't pull that shit on someone you love. And it isn't any way to find love either. That was the last time I ever played that stupid game. I guess at the time Morgan was like self medicating, picking up a bottle to mask the problem. But all you're really doing is adding another.

* * *

Jessica showed up at Allen's grandparents with vodka and beer. As far as parties go, it was lame.

There's something about being surrounded by Hummel figurines, paint-by-numbers, flower-patterned davenports and needlepoint that sucks the life out of an otherwise good time.

When Nicole showed up, it was nice to see her. The love was gone, but the lust lingered, and we ended up in the grandparent's bed. The strangest thing happened in that room, naked in bed with her. Before we even finished—after we'd barely started—I stopped everything and told her I didn't want this, that this wasn't right. She seemed so understanding, so caring. It was the old her. And I felt like shit, because what she didn't realize was I'd stopped because I was still hung up on Morgan, something I didn't even want. This love/lust thing was kicking my ass. All I'd figured out was that one was worth pursuing and the other wasn't, and that differentiating the two was hard as hell.

***

Eddie showed up. He was hard to figure out. He tried to play thug with his Triple F.A.T. Goose, Filas and Chicago Bulls swag, thumping rap in his shitty car stereo. But deep down he was scared of everything. He was a square who fronted hard. But the guy could pull shit on his board most of us couldn't. It was the one thing he wasn't afraid of. There wasn't a gap or set of stairs in town I didn't see him try at least once. When you're like that, it doesn't matter how lame your getup is. You get respect.

The rest of the night was spent babysitting Allen. He'd drank too much early on, filled himself full of vodka and spent hours stuck in that drunken, crying mode with his *"I love you so much, man"* chants, pleading with me to stay with him as he clung to his grandparent's bed.

The party moved to the bedroom where we all sat around Allen like some viewing—an open casket funeral on a handmade quilt that smelled of moth balls and Ben-Gay.

Eddie sat on the corner of the bed in that dumbass coat. I was surprised he was there, honestly.

47

This wasn't his scene, a party with adult beverages. He'd never had a drop in his life. Scared of that, too. But he sat there talking shit, and when he cracked some joke about me screwing anything that moves, I snapped. I dove at him across the bed, grabbed his Triple F.A.T. and cocked back my fist.

"Go ahead," he said. "My boys will be after your ass so fast."

I just stared down at him and thought about his thug boys. He was probably right. They would catch up to me and beat my ass with my own board. But that's not why I didn't swing. I didn't swing because Eddie was my friend. You don't play head games with someone you love, and you don't break a friend's face.

I was learning.

***

I stayed with Allen as the party died and Jessica crawled in bed between us. I thought of Nicole and Morgan and wondered if I ever loved either of them, or were they just pretty faces with good mileage in bed.

Jessica leaned over, kissed me goodnight, then lie on her back and let Allen put his hand down her pants, too drunk for anything else.

Last Dance

1.

We were at Rocco's place: Allen, Begman, Jessica, Vera, and I. He lived with his mom on the third floor of an apartment complex. It was nice. They had a balcony that overlooked a hedge-filled courtyard with a pool in the center that glowed like the moon. We spent most of the time on the balcony, talking. That pool-moon really set a mood, casting shadows that rippled across our faces. Vera turned the conversation to the rapist. Jessica scooted close to me.

"I think his thing is prostitutes."

"If you can just pay for it, why rape?" Rocco asked.

"It's a power trip. Guys like that need to be in control, makes them feel like a man."

"I say we skate downtown, see if we can't spot the guy," Rocco said. "Beat the shit out of him."

"Spot him how?" I asked. "Look for the guy in a ski mask with a chronic boner?"

Everyone laughed, but I didn't think it was funny.

"Who wants a beer?"

We all spoke up. Rocco made a trip to the fridge and came back with a six-pack.

"You allowed to swim at night or is the pool closed?" Begman asked.

"We can go whenever the hell we want...you guys down?"

"We don't have suits," Jessica said.

"So?" Rocco took his shirt off. Vera seemed to like that, and for a second I thought she would join him. She had no problem stripping down. I'd seen her tits before. Maybe we all had. But she just stood and leaned over the balcony rail.

"Is it cold?" She seemed to tease the idea.

"We'll find out." Rocco grabbed the rail and hopped up on it, balancing thirty feet above the courtyard.

"Dude, get down." Begman jumped up and grabbed Rocco's leg.

"I can clear the Leila gap, but you don't think I can clear this?"

"You're not on a board, man. This is from a stand still. And you never cleared the Leila gap."

"It's water, dude."

'If you even make it that far."

We all looked over the edge. No way he could make it. There was at least 12 feet of cement between us and the pool.

"Get down, Rocco. Let's get another beer," I said.

"I can clear that."

"No you can't, Rocco. Get down!" Vera was pleading with him.

Jessica was shaking, her hands covering her mouth, and all I could think about was how beautiful it was to have friends. People you could count on. People who cared.

And then Rocco jumped.

He didn't jump so much as dove. He really believed he could clear the gap and hit the water.

It wasn't that everything went in slow motion, because it didn't. It happened fast. But it's the replays that slow down, like frame-by-frame shots of Rocco diving head first into the pavement. Until I closed my eyes and heard the pops, like a bundle of twigs being snapped over knee.

Rocco made it nowhere near the pool. Neither did the blood that leaked out of him.

2.

It was a long night. Rocco was dead. And if it weren't for the beer, none of us would have slept. We stared out windows listening to the sound of traumatic screams and snapping bones over and over again, trying to make sense out of life.

Vera cried hard. She was really into Rocco and wished she'd told him so, even though she still had her hippie boyfriend. It felt like things wouldn't ever be the same after that. But honestly, I was a little thankful Rocco had distanced himself so much before it happened, became a different person—one that became harder to relate to if you weren't tripping right along with him, or four bowls deep into your high. It made things easier to deal with. It was a selfish thought.

We all crashed at my place. I let Vera and Jessica have the bed. I didn't have a couch so Allen, Begman and I slept on the floor using my dirty laundry as pillows.

* * *

The next morning we discovered Rocco had left his board in Jessica's trunk, so we hit McKinley and took turns sliding his board on the cement benches. Our way of signing it, then deemed it retired and made plans to take it to his mother.

Before we left, we each said a few words about Rocco. Allen broke down and apologized for pissing in his Pepsi, then said "You ain't kiddin', brother. Payback's a bitch."

Homesick

1.

For the next week I hung out with Maurice a lot, mainly at his place. I think his mom liked that, him being around so much. I told him what happened with Rocco. He couldn't believe it, just stared at me and teared up. But I got the feeling it wasn't over Rocco. It was like he wanted to say something but couldn't get it out, then thought better of it.

We binged on fast food and video games. It was nice to get my mind off Rocco and hang out with someone who wasn't there when it happened. Everyone else was a reminder. Even Jessica. Though she'd gone north a few hours away, visiting family for a while. We still talked on the phone every day, and I missed her. I hated that she was up there.

Staying with Maurice was like a vacation from everything else. His mom was cool, just kept to herself, read her bible and drank a ritualistic glass of wine before bed. It probably helped her sleep, seeing how her bed was a lonely place anymore.

One day Maurice and I played catch, right there in his yard with a baseball and mitts. I nearly broke down thinking about his dad being gone. It killed me to think the last time a ball was passed to Maurice was out of his old man's hand. And now it's just me. The hessian.

* * *

For whatever reason, I picked that time to quit smoking cigarettes. I think maybe it gave me something to be proud of. A small accomplishment. A win. Some evidence that I was trying to do something.

Every time I talked to Jessica she'd ask how I was doing with it. She was all kinds of proud when I told her of my success each day. That lasted two weeks.

2.

Jessica met a guy up there. I was really happy for her. She deserved someone. But they only dated for a minute, then she broke it off, said it was a waste of time since she was coming back home at the end of the month. I felt bad for her, but she was right. It would have been a waste of time. Funny how we can never tell until it's too late who's a waste of time and who isn't. You can put life on hold for a whole year dating someone, getting to know them, and then it all falls apart. Your heart is broken and you can't do shit for another half a year without thinking of them, missing them, missing all that wasted time. I suppose with each one we walk away learning something about ourselves, about life, about how to love. Maybe we're all just stepping stones for each other. We're all helping somebody get somewhere. From here to a better there.

3.

With Jessica gone, I was spending a lot of time at the record store around the corner from my place. My friend Stacey worked there. She'd hook me up with promo stuff and we'd sit around making fun of all the bad music customers would buy. I was close-minded then, and probably half the stuff I made fun of I'd end up enjoying one day.

One night after hours, the store had a listening party for the new Jane's Addiction record. There was pizza and beer, and the owner put on the album at high volume while the store full of people stood around and drank and ate and critiqued *Ritual de lo Habitual*.

Afterward, we headed outside to the parking lot. My friend Burgee took a piss against the wall and was confronted by a cop midstream, then given a ticket while the rest of us laughed. I mean, how the hell do you get busted pissing outside?

I stuck around and played hacky sack with a few guys I'd just met. They were good people but a strange group that claimed to be homeless, couch hopping and down on their luck. A car drove by and told us to get a life. One of the guys I was with, a real big guy, threw his arms up at the car like some kind of challenge to come say that to his face. Well, they did. And there were only two of them versus four of us.

The car circled around, parked, and the two got out with an empty bottle of Mountain Dew in each hand—dual-wielding glass clubs glowing green. Most of us kind of stood there, a little shocked, I think, that these guys had the balls. But not the big guy. He strode right toward them, ready to back up the threatening invite he'd given. That's when the first bottle went flying and Big Guy caught it square in the face. It rained green shards every which way, and Big Guy lost every bit of sense he had and stood stunned, blinking away the blood from his eyes. That was it for him. He couldn't have taken another step, let alone thrown a punch. Another bottle was thrown, this time at me. I ran. Like a pussy. We all did, scattered like flies. Except for Big Guy. He still stood dazed, soaked in blood.

The bottle broke at my feet and split my shin open. A battle wound I was kinda proud of, even if I did get it while trying to run. The guys jumped back in the car and took off. They'd made their point. Big Guy didn't walk quite as tall the rest of the night, his pride crushed by a bottle of Dew.

4.

Allen started coming over more just to get drunk. He'd bring 40s with him, and often times we'd end up outside on the curb where he'd puke on the side of the road, his devilock threatening to dip into the puddle he'd made. I started worrying about him, drinking that much. And I couldn't figure out what kept him at it. He had no girl troubles, came from a loving home with great parents, no financial burden. But something was torturing him. Maybe losing Rocco got him. Maybe he thought he deserved the misery after Rocco drank his piss. We've all got our demons, but his were kicking his ass.

Lovesong

1.

Maurice and I were hanging out, walking up and down Capital Avenue. Restaurants, video stores, fast food, dive bars, a head shop, laundromat, and record store. The city had just installed new street lamps along the busiest stretch of road and it gave it this real lively look. They lit up everything. It made the city look bigger than it was, like the place to be.

We ran into Eddie, made small talk, and he asked if we'd heard about Rocco. We said we had and kept it short. We ended up getting the boards out and hitting the two-step handrail up the street. I was chickenshit about handrails and it was the only one I'd try. I'd seen too many bails with nuts being wracked and I never wanted any of that shit.

Maurice got on his board too and worked on what little he could, which was mainly just trying to stay on. I always felt bad about that and thought the poor guy needed a different pastime. Or at least a girlfriend. But he struggled with that too, and as far as I knew was still a virgin.

I made mention that we should head downtown, and Eddie said "Hell no. I'm not gettin' raped." I told you, scared of everything. "I need to get to Brandi's anyway. We're gonna see a movie."

Eddie bailed, and we sat on the curb outside the video store and made fun of him and his rattling stereo as he drove away. A real piece of shit, that thing. We lit up smokes and watched people return their videos. Then I heard a familiar voice behind me.

"Hey, guys!"

It was our friend Skip. Another devilock, but his looked better than Allen's. We hadn't seen a lot of him that summer. He'd been spending his days hanging out in a coffee shop with others, a whole different scene.

"What's up, man?" I flicked my smoke across the parking lot and stood up.

"Just dropped off some vids."

"Skate?"

"Can't. I'm with a friend. She's still inside."

"She?" Maurice and I teased.

"It's not like that. Not even a little."

Then the girl in question walked out. It was the candle store girl. And when she saw me, she lit right up. So did I. We nearly laughed at the irony. We'd only ever traded looks. But they were powerful ones. Not a word had been spoken between us, yet here we were and each of us knew what it meant. That this was inevitable. Destiny, I guess. It sounds cliché, but I'm not sure there's a better word.

Maurice elbowed me. He knew.

"Guys, this is Toni. Toni, this is Jex and Maurice."

"Hi," she said with a wave.

We sat outside the video store and hung out. It was good to see Skip. Even better to finally meet Toni. Maurice ran across the street and treated us to tacos, leaving his board behind to save face. Skip asked how Morgan was doing. I told him I didn't know, hadn't seen her and it'd been over for a while now. He told me he was sorry, that he didn't know. I played it off like it was no big deal, that I was over it, which was close to true. Still, Toni was there and nobody wants to be involved with someone still hung up on the past.

Then Toni asked if we wanted to go for a drive. We ran back to Maurice's car, threw the boards in the trunk, and left in Toni's car with her and Skip. She drove with no real destination. Maurice and I sat in the back, and every once in a while I caught Toni getting a glimpse of me in the rearview. She'd smile. I'd smile back. And I knew there would come a time soon enough where we'd speak openly of the irony and how much we were into each other.

We ended up in the parking lot of a small plaza. It was late, and everything was closed. The back of the plaza butted up against a golf course down a steep hill. At the bottom of the hill was a green. The ninth hole. Maurice brought a 40 wrapped in a brown paper bag and we passed it around while we sat there on the green. The grass was lush and trimmed to perfection, and the moon shined on us like a spotlight on a spongy stage.

The street that ran downhill alongside it was the same street Eddie tightened his trucks, sat on his board and made that hill his bitch. I rode beside him in his car and clocked him going almost thirty-five. By the time we got to the bottom of the hill his face was covered in tears from the wind. Told you, scared of everything but that board.

Skip brought up the recent rapes like it was some kind of ghost story. It made Toni uncomfortable, Maurice too, and things got awkward so I steered the subject to movies and which ones they'd just dropped off. Then a bright light flashed across us and I knew right away it was the cops.

We all looked at the beer. And I'll bet every one of us was trying to think on where the hell we could ditch it. But there was nothing we could do. We were surrounded by nothing more than perfect grass and flashlight beams.

"My dad's gonna kill me," Toni said.

Fortunately, all the cop did was make us empty the 40 there on the ninth hole and take off. Sometimes you luck out like that, when a cop's in a good mood, shows a little empathy. And sometimes they act a dick, just so you know who's boss.

Soon after, Toni dropped us all off at Maurice's car and I grabbed her number. That was the beginning of us.

2.

I spent most of the afternoon with Toni. We drove around, ate some fast food, then headed back to my apartment where we sat and talked. There'd been a cat hanging around my place so I brought it in and gave it the leftover pizza I had in the fridge. The poor thing was starving.

Allen stopped by real quick, knocked on the door. When I opened it he was standing there with a stack of smut mags up to his chin, nearly too many to carry.

"Here, man. Take these...I gotta go."

He pushed the stack into me and I grabbed them before they fell. Then he took off. Holding that shit in front of Toni was embarrassing as hell. Porn was never my thing and Allen knew that, but he was gone before I could call him out.

"Watchya got there?"

She knew exactly what. It was hard to miss. Full-color and glossy. A million shades of pinks and browns.

"These aren't mine."

"Sure they aren't." She smiled.

Allen was messing with me, had to be. I took the smut into the bathroom and tossed it in the shower, turned on the hot water and shut the door. Asshole.

Disintegration

1.

That night after Toni left, I called Maurice and he picked me up. We left for Uncle Don's. Allen, Begman and Vera were already there.

I figured Maurice would drill me for details about Toni, but the ride was quiet. No conversation, no music. Not even NWA. So I picked his brain, asked how he was doing, how his mom was doing. He said he was fine, she was fine. His answers were short. Something was up.

"You alright, man?"

He didn't say anything for a while, and I gave him a minute to construct whatever it was he had to say. By this time we pull up to Don's and he shuts off the car, shifts in his seat and looks at me. We're just sitting there in the dark, staring at each other and he's still figuring it out, taking slow, deep breaths. Then he spills it.

"I'm the rapist."

I didn't even understand what the hell that meant, like the words didn't make a proper sentence no matter how many times I replayed them.

"I'm the one who raped those girls downtown."

I searched his face for a smile, a restrained smirk, waited for him to bust out laughing, tell me he was kidding. But the only thing that moved was his chin. It quivered and dimpled, and his eyes bulged glassy with tears. I didn't know what to say. If he was telling the truth I wanted to put my fist through his face. And if he was lying, it was the most convincing lie I'd ever seen.

I stared out the window and thought about Jessica and how every time the rapes were brought up she'd cower against me like I'd be the one to save her. I thought of Michelle and how bad Maurice wanted her, and what might have happened if they were alone.

Maurice broke down into his hands. His whole body shook, and I watched him like that, hoping to find satisfaction in his suffering. But I didn't. I was numb, my mind flooding with what to do.

"What are you talking about? The hookers?"

Maurice nodded.

"The guy with the ski mask? That's you?"

Nod.

"Bullshit!"

I didn't want to believe it. I wouldn't. Maurice was a mama's boy virgin. A guy who drove us everywhere. Generously shared his cigarettes, his food, his gas. He was a gentle giant who was no threat to a board other than his clumsy feet. He was my friend.

"Why are you telling me this, man? What the hell am I supposed to do with this?"

"I'm so sorry, Jex. I had to tell somebody. It was eating me up."

"It should be! It should be *killing* you, man!"

"Please don't say anything." His face was wet and bloated red.

"Don't say anything? Dude, you're raping women!"

"Not anymore. I'm done, man. I haven't touched anyone else. I swear."

"Three women, dude. Three! And one of them you knew!"

"They're whores."

"I don't give a shit! You can't do that. I can't believe I even have to explain that to you."

I could see Vera through the window of Uncle Don's. She was watching that shitty TV. Her mouth was moving, and I wondered if they were inside right now talking about the fear of being raped, Uncle Don showing off his Bowie knife and how he'd kill a guy again if he had to.

"You can't tell anyone, Jex."

I didn't say anything, just sat and watched Vera's mouth and wondered what was coming out of it.

"Jex...if you tell anyone I swear to God I'll kill myself."

He was looking at me now, letting me know he wasn't kidding. Then he wiped his face, grabbed his keys and got out of the car. Just like that the conversation was over. He left me sitting there with this burden, like a plague passed through the front seats of a Pontiac Grand Am.

He lit a smoke and stood waiting for me, like we were just supposed to go in and crack a few open, surrounded by aging cereal and smiling, naive faces.

I got out and told him to give me a cigarette. I didn't ask. I told him. He handed one over, as well as a lighter with a picture of a large-mouth bass on it, a lure hooked in its mouth. It felt appropriate somehow. Maurice, the barbed lure. Don't take the bite, ladies.

He put his arm around me like some kind of reminder we were friends. Then we walked down the hill to Uncle Don's. The devil by my side.

***

Inside, they'd been talking about Uncle Don's plans for the house. I looked and saw that the back room had been completely gutted, and the entire back wall was gone. Just a gaping hole overlooking the forest ten feet below. It was ridiculous and peaceful.

Uncle Don offered me a beer. I grabbed one and sat down in the back room on the floor and looked out into the woods. Everyone followed me and took a seat. Uncle Don stayed with his TV and I could hear him light a bowl. And for one quick moment I thought about joining him, getting back into that fog of no memory and lazy days. Instead, I downed my beer and grabbed another, slapping a ten on the counter next to the Batman cereal and told Don it's gonna be a long night and to keep them coming.

***

Vera started talking about Rocco and the time him and I were racing for the car after calling shotgun. I stepped on the back of his heel when running and he went down. I'd called him a pussy, told him to walk it off, that we had skating to do. Not knowing I'd ripped a tendon in his leg. He spent a few months in a cast after that.

The room got quiet real quick, uncomfortably so. Then a pair of hands came from behind me and covered my eyes.

"Guess who," a voice said.

It was Jessica. I hadn't expected her for another few days, and when I saw her I nearly started crying. I hugged and kissed her, told her how much she was missed. She knew all about Rocco. I'd kept her updated on the phone. It was great to see her, even helped keep my mind off Maurice most of the night.

***

At one point, Maurice got up to piss, but instead of using the bathroom he climbed down a ladder outside the missing wall and pissed in the woods. When he was coming back up, I whipped out and pissed on him. He cussed me out but that was it. He knew. Nobody questioned any of it. We'd been drinking.

I was quiet that night, and Jessica was exceptionally clingy. Maybe because she'd missed me. Or maybe she sensed the evil in the room. The weight of sin, the stench of it. I hated Maurice for what he'd done. And every smile, chuckle, or kind eye he gave, the hatred grew. I daydreamed of shoving him off the ten-foot drop, of exposing him right there in front of everyone.

I got another beer and hit the bathroom. While I was in there, Jessica came in and playfully asked if she could hold it, help me aim. Then she said: "I love you."

"I love you, too."

"Kiss me."

I did, like always.

"Again."

I did, but was getting annoyed. I had to piss.

"Kiss me again."

This time I stuck my tongue in her mouth and she took it. For me the kiss was passionless and vengeful. For her I think it was something else. Then she took my junk and aimed it at the toilet while I pissed in the marijuana jungle.

2.

I spent the night at Uncle Don's. I didn't want Jessica staying at my place, and I knew that's what she'd want. I'd missed her, but I wanted to be alone. The shit with Maurice was too much and I still wasn't sure what to do.

I slept in the three-wall room on the floor and awoke to birds and rustling leaves.

Uncle Don was in his chair watching TV, zoned out. I went to the bathroom, emptied more of last night's beer and stuck a glob of toothpaste in my mouth, brushed my teeth with my finger. The bathroom door was smeared orange from top to bottom, like it'd been painted with blood, then wiped away, leaving an obvious trace behind.

"Hey, Don. What happened to the door?" After the words came out, I realized it was none of my business and shouldn't have asked. I was prying. These were *his* demons. Don was a private guy, and I knew he dealt with post-traumatic stuff. A part of himself he couldn't ever share with anyone, especially some kid who doesn't know shit about life and death and seeing hell.

Uncle Don turned to me, eyes glazed. His forearm was split with a deep wound that was trying to close but needed stitches. The cut ran through a tattoo he'd gotten in the Army, now defaced. A middle finger to the system that brought the nightmare.

"I think you'd better leave, man. I'm not doing good...and I'm outta meds."

I saw the Bowie knife on the floor near his feet and thought about the time he put his woman in the hospital.

"No problem, Don."

I left and walked to my apartment, thinking about Maurice, wondering if I was ready to send my friend to prison, or see him take his own life.

Prayers for Rain

1.

I called Toni but she wasn't home, so I called Skip and he came over. We sat in my apartment, listening to The Misfits. He saw the smut in my shower, falling apart and scattered like some potpourri of wilted flesh. He seemed interested and did what he could to salvage it. I told him to take it all, and I could tell he was really brainstorming. He loved that shit.

I made us lunch and we grabbed our boards. I needed to stay busy, cut the conversation and get out for a bit. What I really needed was a job, get off this welfare shit and man up. What the hell was the government doing giving away money to the able bodied anyway?

2.

At night, a bunch of us met at the lake. It was Vera's idea. She and Hippie Nathan drove in one car. Me, Allen, Jessica, and Begman in another. And

Eddie in another. He didn't like people driving him around. It freaked him out.

We parked at a cul-de-sac near the beach, then snuck under the gate near the tollbooth. Once we hit the beach, Vera and Nathan stripped down to nothing and ran for the water. Allen, Begman and I followed. Eddie and Jessica stayed on the shore fully clothed while the rest of us enjoyed naked freedom.

It wasn't long before Vera and Nathan took to kissing, then left the water altogether to hit the camper parked at the top of the hill. It was there specifically for lifeguards who worked the beach during open hours, like some dressing-room hangout. Otherwise I don't know what purpose it had, other than taking your woman to after horning it up in the water.

And there we were. Three dudes naked in the water. A real sausage fest. The only other girl there dressed and wanting nothing to do with the water. Suddenly skinny dipping didn't seem like a great idea and we headed for the shore. Before we even got there, headlights flashed through the trees at the top of the hill and Begman yelled, "Cops!"

We scrambled for our clothes, grabbing the first things we could find. I ended up with half my clothes and half Begman's, including his shoes. We ducked down, running through the trees, under the gate and back to the cars without being seen.

It's moments like that, harmless ones, that helped me cope that year. Memories no one should be without. I mean, what's living if you've got no stories to tell?

3.

Toni had the day off so we spent it together. We grabbed some burgers, then drove around, figuring out what to do. We'd both had enough of the mall. I didn't want to pop into Uncle Don's after his recent episode, and I didn't expect her to hang out at McKinley while I skated. So we settled on a movie, sat in the back and talked through the whole thing. There was only one other person there and he wasn't paying attention either. He was reading a book by the light of the screen. Afterward, we made our way to a park and sat on the swings.

As much fun as I was having, I couldn't stop thinking about Maurice. I'd been trying to ignore it, because the more I thought on it, the more I realized every bit of this was on me, that I needed to do something. If Maurice raped another woman how would I live with that? How would *she* live with it? Terrified the rest of her life? Filled with shame and stripped of self worth?

And what if Maurice did as he promised and killed himself? Would it be my fault? What would his mother do? There wasn't anyone I could talk to about it. Not Toni, not Jessica.

While Toni and I were really hitting it off, I wished we had more time invested, that I'd known her longer and that she knew everything about me and my friends, about Maurice and how much of a momma's boy he really was. Then I would tell her and we could figure it out together. Whatever *it* was.

* * *

That night Toni and I snuck onto the beach and sat in the sand and ate French fries and talked about the future. Neither of us had any idea where we were headed or what we wanted, other than kids. We both wanted them one day. And art. We were creative types, with the hopes of using our talents to make a living.

I still hadn't kissed her, which at this point was ridiculous. There was no reason not to. We were boyfriend/girlfriend material, completely compatible. And it may have been premature, but I felt like we were more than just stepping stones.

I longed for the moon to make the night perfect, but the clouds hid it under pillows of bruise that moved quickly toward us.

"It looks like rain," she said.

Quiet flashes of light leaked out from the clouds, reflecting off the lake. And we were quiet with them. Crickets serenaded, the water licked the shore, and my breathing grew heavy as she looked in my eyes with no smile. Just a stare that said if you don't kiss me now there'll never be a better moment.

My stomach sunk and my skin prickled with a nervous heat. Then the first audible strike of lightning pushed me over the edge and I leaned in. She let out a sigh as her lips met mine. It was a kiss well worth the wait and one that seemed to last forever, as the wind picked up, reminding us of the incoming storm.

But we didn't mind the rain. And before long we were sharing a drink of it, buried in the kiss.

Lullaby

1.

The next day, I looked for a job. I put in at least a dozen applications that afternoon. One place hired me on the spot. Just so long as I cut my hair. I said no thanks. I knew I'd either look back one day and think that was a dumbass move, or I'd be proud of the old me. Dignity and all that.

I made plans to hang out with Toni that night, show her off to my friends. Everyone was going to the Arboretum. It was beautiful there at night, like a hilly golf course with no holes, peppered with trees, bushes, and flowers. In the middle of it all was a museum that kept odd hours, only open a few days a week. Right inside was a giant stuffed moose, big as a dinosaur. But I'd been there recently and it didn't seem so big anymore. Funny how time changes perspective.

Everyone was already there by the time we pulled up, except for Maurice. I introduced Toni to everyone. I was most excited about her meeting Jessica. My best friend. But Jessica was cold toward her, rude even. It was embarrassing. I'd told Toni all about her. We'd even talked of playing matchmaker with a friend of hers and future double dates. But Jessica pulled her alpha bullshit.

We sat in the grass and drank beer. No one brought up Rocco or hookers getting raped, and other than Jessica's attitude, it was a good night.

Toni had to pee so I walked her over to a bush near her car and waited while she went. Afterward, she kissed me and told me she liked my friends. She didn't mention anything about Jessica being an asshole. Then she took my hand and led me to the car. We climbed inside and kissed. Mastering it, perfecting it, exploring each other's bodies. We slowed down before it went further. Neither of us wanted our first time together to be in a car while my friends gathered forty feet away. So we talked, and I held her while the windows remained fogged.

* * *

A rapid pounding on the driver's side window scared us both. Toni screamed, startling me all the more. Her scream was an awful sound that was quick and eaten by the car's interior, and I instantly thought of Maurice and what he'd done and what every girl must have gone through—still going through—because of my asshole friend, and told myself he would never do it again. I would make sure of it.

A light flashed in my eyes through the fogged glass. I cracked the window and let a million passionate breaths escape. A cop stood outside the car, flashlight in hand, telling us to take it somewhere else.

By that time, everyone had left. Toni dropped me off and said she'd see me tomorrow after work. I wanted her to stay but I wanted something different out of us. Something more than sex. And it felt good taking it slow, getting to know each other on another level. I was in no hurry and neither was she.

After she dropped me off, I walked to the payphone up the street and made a call to the police, anonymously. I told them everything I knew and where to find Maurice. I hung up the phone in tears. I had to keep reminding myself this was Maurice's fault, not mine. But it didn't help, and the burden I'd been carrying was replaced by one where I sent my friend to prison, his mother left alone in an empty house.

***

Jessica showed up soon after I went to bed. She had a key and let herself in, climbed into bed.

"I don't like her," she whispered.

I ignored her and fell asleep. This time with my arms around myself.

* * *

I woke up with an erection. Not uncommon by any means, but Jessica's hand was wrapped around it. I pushed her hand away and got out of bed, got dressed.

"Why don't you like Toni?"

"I don't like her hair, all teased out, like some hessian chick."

I looked at Jessica's hair, towering above her head in full Robert Smith glory. "You're kidding, right?"

"And her legs are too skinny. They don't match her tits."

"So you'd like her if she looked more like you?"

"You don't have to get defensive."

"You don't even know her." I went to the kitchen and Jessica followed.

"Neither do you!"

I poured a bowl of cereal and stared at the box, begging the text for distraction.

"She's gonna break your heart, just like Morgan."

I didn't say anything and read about nutritional facts and about the prize inside the box.

"Hey." She ran her fingers through my hair. "I'm just looking out for you...I love you."

Still I said nothing.

94

"I love you."

"Love you, too."

"Let's do something fun today! Like get drunk before noon and make fun of shoppers."

"I've got plans with Toni."

"When?"

"Around six."

"Shit, we've got all day."

"I'm not getting drunk before noon."

"Then let's go see a movie."

"Not in the mood."

"McKinley?"

"Sorry, Jess. I just don't feel like doing anything."

"Then let's drive around and you can stare out the window and wallow or whatever."

So that's what we did. And I spent the time outside the window, feeling guilty for my freedom and wondering if Maurice was still at home or if he'd already spent his last night there, and about Toni and whether or not she really would break my heart.

We ended up in a parking lot that overlooked a meadow. It shined like gold under the sun. I pictured Toni and I holding hands, running through it, and knew I was screwed. I was already in deep and couldn't slow down.

Jessica and I sat on the hood of her car, The Cure preaching somber words I didn't want to hear. Then she held my cheek and pulled my face toward hers.

"I love you," she said.

"I love you, too." I forced a smile.

"No...I mean I love you."

"I know."

"No, Jex...I'm in love with you."

Something cracked in that moment, a fragile thing so easily broken. And right then I realized she'd been holding those words forever, and now that they were out, there was no more us. We had cracked and lay broken in the parking lot. And I saw how frail and unstable we were together. A thin clay pot held by a glue that was never meant to last. Not through words like that.

Pictures of You

1.

For the next few months I stayed away from everyone but Toni. We were inseparable and the only thing that kept me going. She was good for me, even kept me sober. Not because she insisted but because she made life worth living without a crutch. My friends would call something like that being pussy whipped. I didn't look at it like that. I mean, if we're not searching for someone to make us better people, to excel in life, then what in the hell are we doing?

For the first time in my life I felt like I had a grasp on love versus lust. It can be a very fine line. One that's impossible to see. Until you start questioning where the selfishness went, the bits of jealousy and the worry. Because they're gone now.

***

Allen stopped by a few times. The first time was to see if I'd heard about Maurice, that he was in jail facing rape charges and could I believe that because he sure couldn't and thought we should find the real guy. I told him nothing I knew and kept the burden to myself. I told him if he really wanted to help then check on Maurice's mom from time to time, something I should have been doing, but I couldn't bear to face her. Not yet.

***

More than a few times I came home to notes on my door from Jessica. Some were threatening letters addressed to Toni, which I never showed her. Some simply said, "I love you." Others were paragraphs of "Remember when we...?" It was sad. The notes were manipulative and selfish and heartbreaking. I wanted Jessica to be happy for me. But she was like an ex now, full of bitterness and resentment.

She'd call, too. But I never took the calls. It was a shitty thing to do but I couldn't face her either. There was a lot of guilt there. Had I led her on? I guess I felt like this kind of thing was supposed to happen the other way around. The guy with the burning desire, wanting nothing more than to be with the naive girl who can't see the signs. There was a lot of hindsight. A lot of guilt and a lot of missing. I missed what we had.

2.

Toni and I snuck into a karaoke bar one night. They were serving free tacos, so we filled up and she taught me how to squirt water between my teeth. By the time we left we were both soaked.

On the way back to my place, a pickup truck in front of us with a couple of jocks in the back threw full cans of beer at our windshield. Not a single one hit thanks to Toni's swerving skills, but shit got scary for a minute.

We stopped at the store and bought funny sunglasses, wore them at night. We looked like bugs driving cars and laughed whenever we looked in the mirror. Toni was a beautiful bug, biting her lip in an insecure smile that said she'd lived her whole life not seeing the beauty I did.

Up ahead, a cop had a truck pulled over, the driver in handcuffs. We slowed down and realized it was the jocks who'd thrown the beer. We slowed even more so they could get a good, long look at our saluting fingers and teeth-baring smiles.

3.

I found myself skating a lot less. The city had torn down McKinley, and everywhere else was just a reminder that this was as good as it got: Shitty curbs, handrails, impossible gaps, gravel-filled banks that could never launch us as high or as far as McKinley's humps. It was like settling for one night stands instead of true love.

We built a half pipe in Allen's backyard, but it was small and I hated skating vert. Or maybe I was outgrowing it all. Skating all day, no job, alcoholic interludes. Maybe I was maturing. Between Rocco's death, Maurice's confession, finding Toni, and the demise of McKinley, my perspective was changing.

4.

Toni stayed at my place a lot. We eventually named the cat I'd taken in. Cherienne. She'd sleep on the windowsill next to the bed, watching us fall in love.

I never said anything to Toni, but sometimes I'd see Jessica drive by. I could hear the low hum of The Cure as she'd slowly pass. Finally, I decided the next time she called I would answer, let her say whatever she needed and end it.

It didn't take long. Jessica called one night while Toni was at work. She always called when Toni wasn't there, like she knew. She was excited to hear my voice, to have me answer her call. She begged me to speak with her in person and I agreed to. Within minutes she was at my place. She hugged me and was trembling, whispering that she loved me. Then she tried to kiss me and I pulled away.

Her eyes were hazel pits of sadness and despair. Melancholy and fear.

"Let's go to the lake," she said.

"We can't do this anymore, Jessica. You know that, right?"

"Just one more time. Our last dance together."

I wanted to argue but couldn't. The way things had ended was ugly. The way I avoided her, the desperate way she pursued me. I owed her that much. I grabbed my keys and smokes and we left for the lake.

The Same Deep Water as You

1.

The moon was in full bloom and brilliant, the occasional cloud teasing cover. It was the kind of moon I longed for when I first kissed Toni.

Jessica and I sat in the sand and talked. She was feeling out my relationship with Toni, measuring my dedication, asking about her, my favorite things, my dislikes—none of which I had. Some of her questions were inappropriate and troubling, considering the circumstances between us.

"Does she please you in bed? Is her tongue like mine? Does she get wet at the sound of your voice?"

Our discussion went nowhere. She blurted unfair comparisons and guilt-fed declarations, all given with irrational jealousy. I recognized no friend in Jessica and wondered just how much of her time with me was lust disguised as friendship. And were we ever really friends?

There was a quiet lull in conversation where we both seemed to be reflecting. It felt like waiting out the rest of a bad movie, one I just as soon walk out on. And then Jessica took off her clothes, there on the beach, under the moon.

I kept my eyes fixed on the still water. "Jess, put your clothes back on."

She dropped to her knees, behind a wall of tears, and touched my face.

"Kiss me goodbye." She leaned in with salty, wet lips and kissed me, then stood and headed for the water.

"We should get going, Jess."

She waded out until her breasts were under the silver-blue water, then turned and faced me.

I couldn't hear the words, but I saw them mouthed. Words that had run their course. And then something twinkled in her hand as she brought it swiftly across each wrist.

The image played in my mind, trying to interpret it, with the most ghastly thoughts racing through. Until blood pooled like spilled ink around her as she went under.

I ripped off my shoes and ran for the lake, the entire year playing through my head, a reel-to-reel montage complete with a haunting soundtrack. The screaming of her name seemed to come from another's mouth as it echoed across the lake.

I dove in fully clothed, panic stricken as I stood waist deep, searching for any sign of her. The sway of jet black hair, a glimpse of ivory skin. Or even a cloudy trail of crimson. But the moon rode the rippling waves, hiding my dear friend under them. A kaleidoscope of azure and scarlet impossible to see through.

Again, I dove in the water, feeling my way forward, deeper. My eyes and mouth filled with the senseless letting of blood, diluted by a lake meant for pleasant memories. I sprung for air, then continued the effort, that otherworldly scream carrying across the lake still.

I swam frantically, my arms a windmill that reached for hope, to touch what I desperately prayed for, until they grew stiff against the dense water. I rose and listened for a high-pitched chuckle, a sign that it's all been a joke. But there was only quiet. Except for the scream that wouldn't cease, a howl that hung mercilessly in my ears as my mouth launched it.

I made my way to the shore and hawkeyed the water, watching it fall still into the serene sheet of glass it was only ten minutes before.

For hours I watched the lake, holding tight to Jessica's clothes, their scent a ghost left behind. And I made a foolish deal with death that if only Jessica would surface, aware and full of life, I would let her love me, that I would love her back. That I would sacrifice all for her selfish breath again, to be here for me, to build more memories. All with our own soundtrack.

But no deal was made.

2.

I woke before the sun, Jessica's eggshell eyes watching as I slept.

I couldn't move.

My friend's bloated body had made its way to the shore. Not stalled by the hanging branch of a willow or wrapped in a lily pad grave, but there on the shore, head in the sand, her legs still swimming a weak current. She shone white under the dying moon. Pale and lifeless.

I couldn't move.

I couldn't reach her eyes to close them, so I shut my own. I still saw her. I bawled with my face in the sand, clawing the ground with a thousand regrets, while the birds announced a new day approaching.

I moved.

I sat and watched the tree line across the lake as the sky behind it changed its hue. Jessica lie naked and undeserving, mouth agape. Never to utter the words again. I gathered her clothes and joined her near the water, covering her.

"I loved you, too."

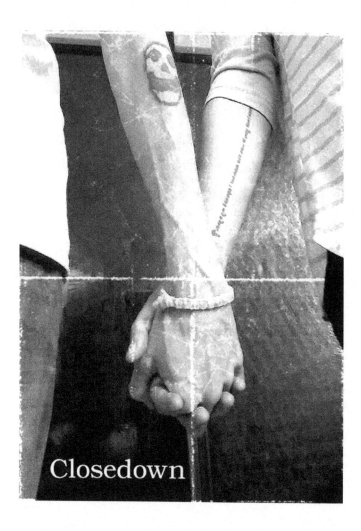

Closedown

My first inclination was to hide away from the rest of the world, even from Toni. I was afraid the next time I kissed her I would think of Jessica, that the guilt of loving Toni would be too much to bear, that things would be tainted now and it would be too easy to fall into a drunken spell of self pity.

Instead, I did the opposite. I clung to Toni desperately, feeling the sting of vulnerability. But her selflessness knew no bounds. And even when I cried for Jessica, for the loss of her friendship, for the loss of her life, Toni held tight to me and displayed an empathy I'd never seen before. There was no selfishness. No jealousy.

This was love. And if Toni turned out to be a stepping stone herself, it would be one that carried me for miles, teaching me more than I'd ever need. But the ground that she and I were planted on was firm and unshakeable, with Jessica, in some curiously poignant way, having been the stone to secure such a foundation. With a soundtrack I'll never forget.

Disclaimer: There's nothing romantic about taking your own life. Nothing beautiful. There is no statement to be made stronger than any you could make while alive. So, scream from the hilltops. Direct your rage, your hurt, and your loneliness in a positive way. And if you're ever feeling like you can't go on, find help. You are not alone. The world needs you! Every bit of you.

Gratitude: Thank you to my wife, Mary, Mark Matthews, John Boden, Zach McCain for the beautiful cover, Cyndie Randall, Lydia Capuano, McKinley School (R.I.P.), Battle Creek, Broken Trust, The Sinatras, 1990, Gonzo, Rock Café Records and Tapes. My patreons: M. Louise, Dan Padavona, Connie McNeil Bracke, Shannon Everyday, Steve Gracin, Linda Lee, Shaun Hupp, Michael Perez, Tim Feely, Dyane Hendershot, George "Book Monster" Ranson, Liane Abe, Steven Gomzi, Dean Watts, Katrina Hughes, Karlee "A Stranger Dream", Mindi Snyder, Night Worms (Sadie Hartmann & Ashley Saywers), Patti Smeltzer, and Diamond Kennedy. But most of all Team ICE, The Cure, and Julie.

Photography: Mary Lutzke, Chad Lutzke, Scott Dix, Nick Ortloff, Mittendazzle, James Richmond, and Steve Soblick

Chad lives in Michigan with his wife and children. For over two decades, he has been a contributor to several different outlets in the independent music and film scene, offering articles, reviews, and artwork. He has written for Famous Monsters of Filmland, Rue Morgue, Cemetery Dance, and Scream magazine. He's had a few dozen stories published, and some of his books include: OF FOSTER HOMES & FLIES, WALLFLOWER, STIRRING THE SHEETS, SKULLFACE BOY, and OUT BEHIND THE BARN co-written with John Boden. Lutzke's work has been praised by authors Jack Ketchum, Stephen Graham Jones, James Newman, Cemetery Dance, and his own mother.

To join my VIP reader list and be included in all future giveaways, visit www.chadlutzke.com

OF FOSTER HOMES
AND FLIES

"Original, touching coming of age."
- Jack Ketchum, author of The Girl Next Door

CHAD LUTZKE

A neglected 12-year-old boy does nothing to report the death of his mother in order to compete in a spelling bee. A tragic coming-of-age tale of horror and drama in the setting of a hot New Orleans summer.

"My name is Levi. I'm 16. I've got a skull for a face. And here's how shit went down."

Having never been outside the walls of Gramm Jones Foster Care Facility, sixteen-year-old Levi leaves in the middle of the night with an empty backpack and a newfound lust for life. A journey that leads him into the arms of delusional newlyweds, drunkards, polygamists, the dangerous, and the batshit crazy. His destination? Hermosa Beach, California where he's told there is another like him, with the face of a skull.

A coming-of-age road trip filled with surreal Lynch-ian encounters exploring the dark, the disturbing, and the lonely in a 1980s world—an epic venture for one disfigured boy struggling to find his place in the world.

After an encounter with a homeless man, a high school graduate becomes obsessed with the idea of doing heroin, challenging himself to try it just once. A bleak tale of addiction, delusion, and flowers.

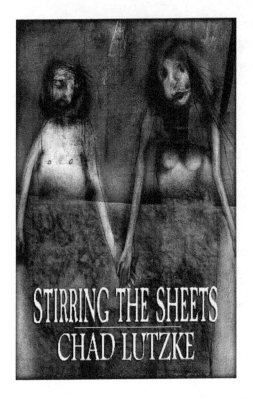

STIRRING THE SHEETS

CHAD LUTZKE

An elderly funeral home worker, struggling with the loss of his wife, finds an unnatural attraction to a corpse at work resembling his late bride in her younger years.

A story of desperation, loneliness and letting go.

The boys crept to the window and watched as Miss Maggie carried the long bundle into the barn, the weight of it stooping her aging back. Rafter lights spilled from the barn doors and Davey saw an arm fall from the canvas-wrapped parcel. He smiled.

"She got someone!"

Both children grinned and settled in their beds, eyes fixed to the ceiling.

This was family growth.